FOR
GARY
♡

Delphine Durand

THE FLOPS

Translated from the French
by Sarah Klinger and Delphine Durand

ENCHANTED LION BOOKS
NEW YORK

TABLE OF CONTENTS

The Flops

The basic Flop
(The classic Flop)

~ Flopus Classicus ~

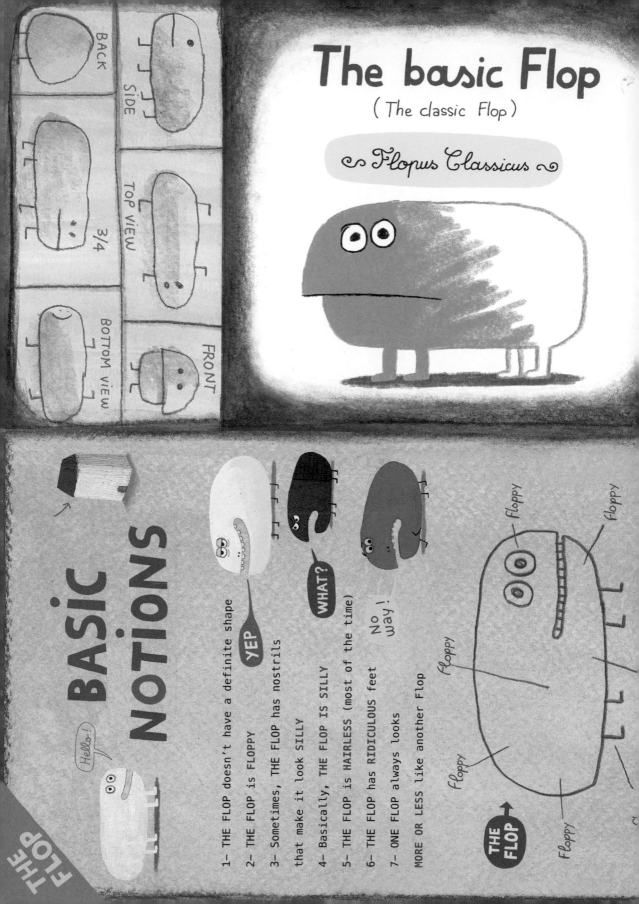

BACK · SIDE · 3/4 · TOP VIEW · BOTTOM VIEW · FRONT

BASIC NOTIONS

Hello!

1— THE FLOP doesn't have a definite shape

2— THE FLOP is FLOPPY · YEP

3— Sometimes, THE FLOP has nostrils that make it look SILLY · WHAT?

4— Basically, THE FLOP IS SILLY

5— THE FLOP is HAIRLESS (most of the time) · No way!

6— THE FLOP has RIDICULOUS feet

7— ONE FLOP always looks MORE OR LESS like another Flop

floppy · floppy · floppy · floppy · floppy · floppy

THE FLOP

GIANT TASMANIAN FLOP

VERY RARE FLOPS

FOUR-EYED FLOP

SQUATTING FLOP

Mmmph

TA-DA!

MAGIC FLOP

SQUARE FLOP

ZOMBIE FLOP

ains

CHAMELEON FLOP

NOTHING FLOP

What do you mean, nothing?

LONGHAIRED FLOP

Hiccup

TIPSY FLOP

POETIC FLOP

LONG-LEGGED
FLOP

11

FIG. 226.B: The Flop can teleport, but it can't control where it ends up.

Chapter 1

THE FLOP

General characteristics

Hello!

THE FLOP can do this:

HOWEVER: It can't make phone calls on its own.

THE FLOP is FLEXIBLE

Hi, there!

Whoa! This is really working!
But wait, could I be dreaming?

Diagram .129.C

FOR EXAMPLE:

You can squish the FLOP into a box. It's fine.

Diagram .163.A

If you want to slide one under a door:

It's fine.

DOOR

GROUND   FIG.1

LOOK!

THE FLOP has various facial expressions.

Please note the subtle differences:

DOUBTFUL FLOP

SKEPTICAL FLOP

EMBARRASSED FLOP

BEWILDERED FLOP

CONFUSED FLOP

WORRIED FLOP

GOOD TO KNOW:

The FLOP likes to have its chin scratched.

THE FLOP does silly things.

Check out my new sneakers!

Sometimes the FLOP says **SILLY THINGS:**

* LET US OBSERVE THIS ANCESTRAL RITUAL:

the Flop Pyramid

But then again, sometimes:

THE FLOP is unflappable

EXAMPLE

Exactly!

Chomp!

Meh...

Flip off.

Flops are homebodies.
Too much adventure
makes them uneasy.

COMMUNICATING WITH THE FLOP

(can be quite a challenge)

FLOP BIOLOGY

The complex Flop and the simple Flop: Fig. 649 c bis

FLOP ANATOMY

Many studies suggest that there are simple Flops and complex Flops.

Is there someone inside the FLOP?

North-Northeast direction clear!

Obstruction at nine o'clock!

U-turn!

Keep going, to the left!

It remains a question to this day...

Hi there!

perspective

SOME FLOPS HAVE A LITTLE BAG

And together, they wander around happily.

Doo-padoom...

Let's find out what's inside:

Whoa, weird! A bone!

So what. Mind your own business!

The Flop lives in perfect harmony with nature.

When walking through the woods, you'd never suspect that just below, maybe, a Flop is playing on his tablet.

FLOPS USE THEIR LITTLE PAWS TO DIG HOLES

like this

and like this

YEAH yeah

we get it!

...hey dig subterranean ...ens that keep them ...warm during the winter.

FLOPS eat little colored balls that they find underground.

This Flop ate too much and can't leave its burrow

Ugh...!

The Flopette

THE FEMALE FLOP is called a FLOPETTE

The Flopette lays her eggs and sits on them. For three days.

THE FLOPETTE'S EGGS ARE SOFT

:) :|

NEWBORN FLOPS DON'T HAVE LEGS

...h!

Oh no!

he he

FIG. 923A: Flop Houses

Chapter 2

Cousin to the flop:

THE TUFF

The Tuff is a type of Flop, but tough.

(Also known as: The **TUFF-FLOP**)

Step 1: Learn how to tell **the Flop** from **the Non-Flop**:

The **FLOP**:

The **NON-FLOP**:

<u>Above all</u>: **DO NOT CONFUSE**:

and

flop ≠ non-flop

the square Flop

THE TUFF (or Tuff-Flop)

THE TUFF

HOW TO TELL THEM APART:

— <u>Poke them to see if they're soft</u>

WHOA!

When poked, the **square flop** is: **SOFT**.

When poked, a *tuff* is: **HARD!**

Note: Do not over-poke. It's annoying.

The Tuff can't sit down

Ugh...

he he

Whereas the Flop can.

Definitely do not confuse the **Tuff-Flop** with the **Unfloppy-Flop.**

...me again?

S'cuse me ?

WHAT?

Huh?

No Kidding?

And beware of imposters.

non-Flop that looks like the Flop. Or rather the Tuff.

That is to say the Floppy-Tuff.

Remember: there are always exceptions to the rules.

semi =Tuff, semi-Flop = TUFFYFLOP

The Tuff in perspective

tuff

half un-floppy Flop

Oh no!

the VERY floppy Flop

tuff

tuff

tuff

tuff

you ok ?

HUMPH

the floppiest flop

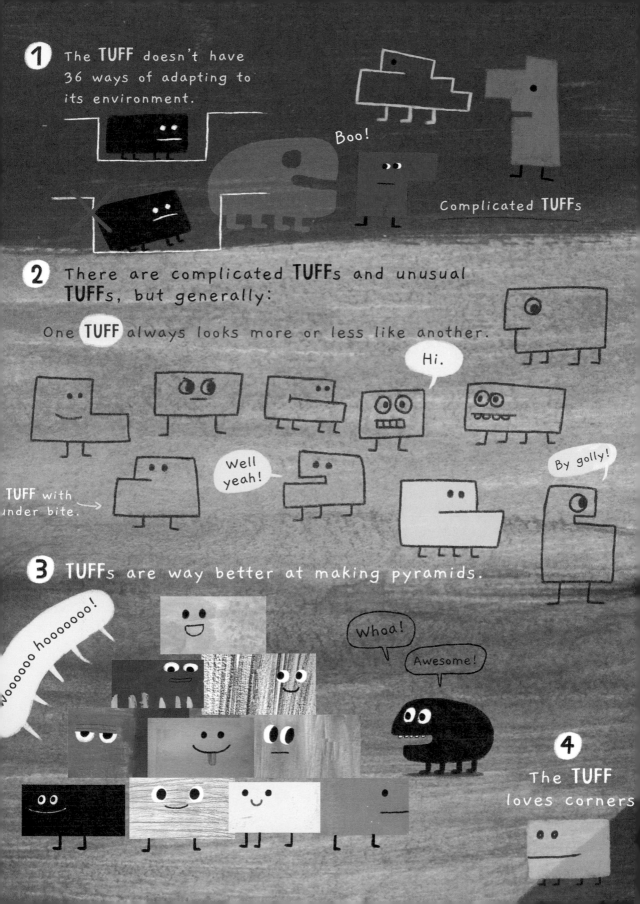

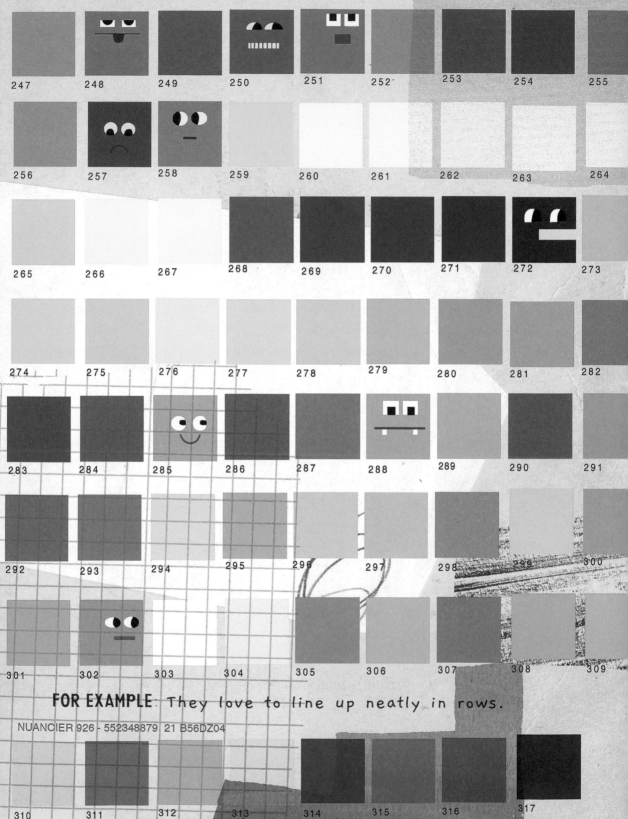

NOTE 28 - FIG. 31C TUFFs are very organized.

247 248 249 250 251 252 253 254 255

256 257 258 259 260 261 262 263 264

265 266 267 268 269 270 271 272 273

274 275 276 277 278 279 280 281 282

283 284 285 286 287 288 289 290 291

292 293 294 295 296 297 298 299 300

301 302 303 304 305 306 307 308 309

FOR EXAMPLE: They love to line up neatly in rows.

NUANCIER 926 - 552348879 21 B56DZ04

310 311 312 313 314 315 316 317

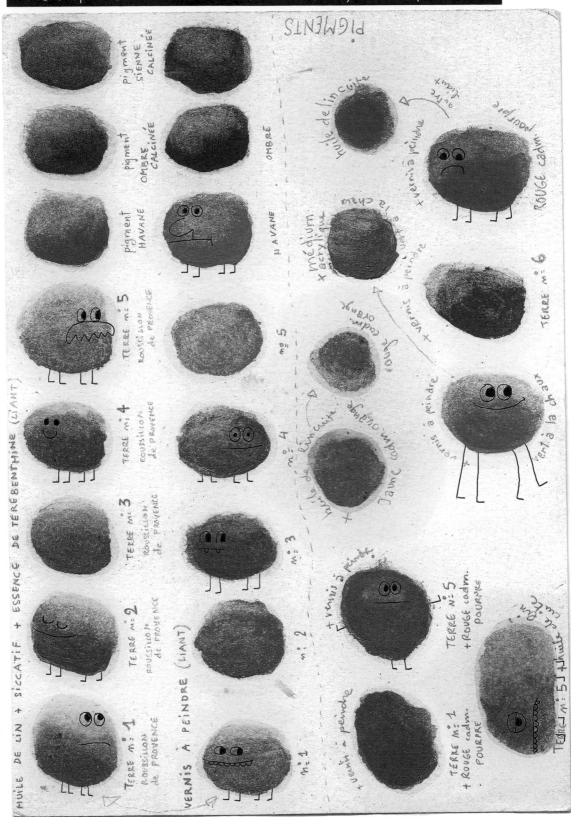

PLEASE NOTE: Sometimes the Tuff will dress up like the Flop.

FLOPPY JOE and PHILIP FLOP

NOTE 265C, FIG 8: Flops like to get together at dusk.

HOW TO SPOT THE FLOP

Pay close attention to the differences between the Flop and the Non-Flop

IMPORTANT:

You must be very careful about how you hold the Flop.

NO

YES

You may dress the **FLOP** in wintertime...

but not in your own clothing.

For when it's cold

For when it's freezing

Energy Juice

FLOP APPAREL

Flop clothing exists and can be found.

Shoes

Flop sandals

IF YOU HAVE A FURRY FLOP:

Don't shave it and then put it in clothes:
There's no point to that.

DON'T DO THIS EITHER . IT'S DUMB.

Longhaired FLOPS
Require more care:

1) Carefully comb to remove all tangles.

2) After, the choice is yours. Let your creativity be your guide.

WHAT TO DO iF THE FLOP ST~~IN~~KS?

smells bad

Do not feed garlic to the **FLOP**

Do not bathe the **FLOP**:
It will sink. Instead,
wipe it down with a damp
sponge* or a clean cloth.

NOTE: You can moisture
your **FLOP** with hair oil

<u>A WELL-OILED FLOP
iS BEST</u>

*No soap

<u>DON'T DO DUMB</u> THINGS TO YOUR <u>**FLOP**</u>

HEY!

That's my derriere

Do not subject
it to stressful
situations.

Do not annoy your FLOP.
Your FLOP is not a cat.

Meow

OR A DOG

Come on!
Go fetch your ball!

We need to talk.

The FLOP is not a cozy chair, either.

THE FLOP REQUIRES ENTERTAINMENT

Let them watch a little TV every once in a while.

Choose special FLOP programing or they'll tune out.

SOMETIMES the FLOP WILL SURPRISE YOU

Beep beep !

Falalalala !

BUT MOST OF THE TIME, NOTHING WILL HAPPEN

*Avoid staring at the FLOP. It makes them nervous.

WATCH OUT!

When the Flop is not in its natural habitat, it may feel miserable and cope by stuffing itself.

crunch
crunch
crunch

And before you know it, you'll have an ENORMOUS FLOP!

FIG. 54C: Example of a FLOP that can no longer flip itself over.

This can lead to complications.

TO AVOID THIS:

PFFFF...

Exercise the Flop regularly.

Fig.12

REMINDER: The flop can't ride a bicycle.

Offer it fun, educational activities.

TAKE CARE OF YOUR <u>FLOP</u>

Give it a little quiet place of its own.

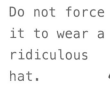

Find a suitable shape

Do not put your Flop
under a cheese dome.

Do not force
it to wear a
ridiculous
hat.

AND ABOVE ALL:
*Give your Flop
lots of hugs.*

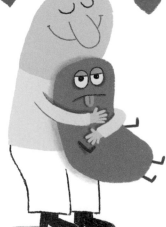

Splurge on a <u>Flop Tree</u>

thanks!

FiNAL iNSTRUCTiONS

What to do if your Flop behaves strangely?

DETERMiNE THE CAUSE:
- Have you put it in an uncomfortable situation?
- Has it swallowed something it shouldn't have?
- Have you forgotten to administer its drops?

WHATEVER THE CASE:

- ~~Dip it in water~~
- ~~Dip it in oil~~
→ ~~it will make~~ NO-NO-NO-NO

Don't react right away.
That could make the problem worse.
Be patient.
These things usually sort themselves out. →

In conclusion, OWNING A FLOP is:

- ☐ interesting
- ☐ inappropriate
- ☐ TBD
- ☐ don't know
- ☐ terrific
- ☐ bizarre

- ☐ so cool
- ☐ complicated
- ☐ rather not to say
- ☐ dumb
- ☐ nice enough
- ☐ awesome

* Check any and all boxes that apply

www.enchantedlion.com

First English-language edition published in 2019 by Enchanted Lion Books,
67 West Street, 317A, Brooklyn, NY 11222
Translated from the French by Sarah Klinger and Delphine Durand
Copyright © 2019 by Enchanted Lion Books for the English-language text
Production and layout of US edition: Julie Kwon
Originally published in France in 2015 as "Les Mous"
Copyright © 2015 by Editions du Rouergue
All rights reserved under International and Pan-American Copyright Conventions
A CIP record is on file with the Library of Congress
ISBN 978-1-59270-260-2

Printed in China by RR Donnelley Asia Printing Solutions Ltd.

10 9 8 7 6 5 4 3 2 1

The rocks on page 44 were painted with Chamo. Thanks for the permission to use the photo.